THE SURVIVORSHIP NET

THE SURVIVORSHIP NET

A Parable for the Family, Friends, and Caregivers of People with Cancer

Written by Jim Owens

Illustrated by Bill Cass

**Foreword by
Lance Armstrong**

American Cancer Society

Published by the American Cancer Society
Health Promotions
250 Williams Street NW
Atlanta, Georgia 30303 USA
Copyright ©2010 American Cancer Society

For permission to reprint any materials from this publication, contact the publisher at
permissionrequest@cancer.org.

Manufactured by RR Donnelley
Manufactured in Reynosa, Mexico, in February 2010
Job# 80092

Printed in Mexico

Design and composition by Martha Benoit

5 4 3 2 1   10 11 12 13 14

Library of Congress Cataloging-in-Publication Data
Owens, James R, 1962–2009.
The survivorship net: a parable for the family, friends, and caregivers of people with cancer/by Jim Owens; illustrated by Bill Cass; with a foreword by Lance Armstrong.
p. cm.
ISBN-13: 978-1-60443-018-9 (hardcover: alk. paper)
ISBN-10: 1-60443-018-4 (hardcover: alk. paper)
1. Owens, James R, 1962–2009—Health—Juvenile literature. 2. Brain—Tumors—Patients—Biography —Juvenile literature. 3. Brain—Tumors—Patients—Family relationships—Juvenile literature. I. Cass, Bill, ill. II. Title.
RC280.B7094 2010
362.196'994810092—dc22
[B]
2009045023

AMERICAN CANCER SOCIETY
Strategic Director, Content: Chuck Westbrook
Director, Cancer Information: Terri Ades, DNP, FNP-BC, AOCN
Director, Book Publishing: Len Boswell
Managing Editor, Books: Rebecca Teaff, MA
Books Editor: Jill Russell
Book Publishing Coordinator: Vanika Jordan, MSPub
Editorial Assistant, Books: Amy Rovere

For more information about cancer, contact your American Cancer Society at
800-227-2345 or **cancer.org**.
Quantity discounts on bulk purchases of this book are available. For information, please contact the American Cancer Society, Health Promotions Publishing, 250 Williams Street NW, Atlanta, GA 30303-1002, or send an e-mail to **trade.sales@cancer.org**.

~ For Max ~
the best boy in the whole world

Foreword

A book written by a dad who rides bikes, about how to tell his son he has cancer. I didn't write this book, but I'm glad my dear friend Jim did.

Riding a bike is thought to be so easy. . ."even a kid can do it." Telling your own child you have cancer may be the most difficult thing anyone could imagine having to do. Well, Jim did it. He did both. He rode his bike across the country to inspire hope in others, and he wrote this book that talked to his son, and all of us, about the fear and challenges cancer brings into our lives. Jim did this all with classic Minnesota mettle— stabilizing his bike amid tremors, putting that same calm determination into words, reaching within, extending himself to others, showing us what could be done.

Showing us a will and a way.

This book is a story told to a child—told from a man who could outsmile most kids, through most circumstances, and keep pedaling along the way. It's filled with some familiar characters, creating a make-believe world that is all too real for people affected by cancer. It's a parable, but also a story I've seen firsthand.

If you're faced with a life and death challenge, or maybe just a small one, give it a read. Or better yet, read it to a kid and have a talk along with it. Take that kid on a bike ride, lend a hand, grab a little thread to help weave someone else's net.

And to my friend Jim: I've seen you lead this circus—from hospital to hospital, from town to town. It may require a net, but it is your circus master spirit that made us all spin, ride, fly, and smile along with you. If there is a tougher bike rider or braver cancer patient out there, I've not met them. As a storyteller, you covered ground that we all find so hard to put into words with simple ones that remind us all of how precious life, friends, and family are.

May this book serve us all as a guide to living life through the eyes of a child in the toughest of times.

Thank you, Jim. Thank you on behalf of all the dads, kids, and cancer patients in the world.

Ride on and Livestrong.

Lance Armstrong

People were out and about in Max's neighborhood. It was a sunny, beautiful summer day, the kind of day that was perfect for walking the dog, taking a bike ride, or working in the garden.

Max, however, was glumly sitting in his room. He was worried. His dad was sick with something called cancer. Dad was tired a lot, he had lost his hair, and he hardly ever had the energy to play with Max anymore.

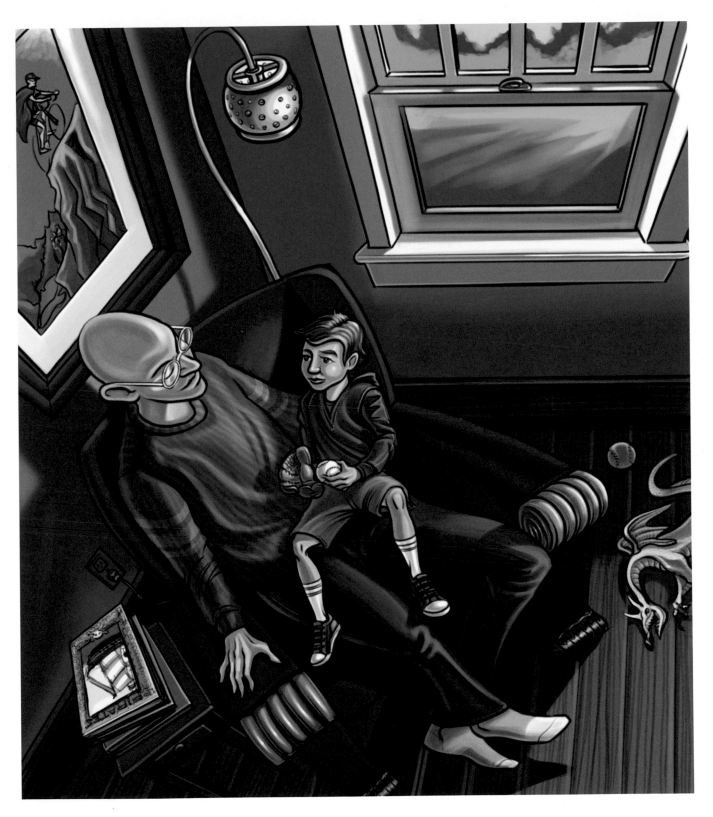

Dad went inside Max's room. He put his hand on his son's shoulder and sat down in the big, comfy chair. Maybe, he thought, a story would help Max understand how cancer can turn your life upside down—for a little while anyway. "Let me tell you a story," he said. And Max climbed into his lap to listen.

So began the story…

A long time ago in the town of Sweetwater, a shimmering blue and yellow tent would appear on the first day of summer at the top of Big Hill. It signaled that The J. J. Owens Roundbottom Circus was back in town. The circus could be seen from miles away, in every direction. Every show would sell out. Excitement rippled in the air!

People would come from far and wide to see the greatest show on earth and be greeted by the booming voice of the Ringmaster, James J. Owens. Before every show, Ringmaster Owens would greet everyone with his deep laugh, hearty handshake, and sparkling blue eyes full of joy.

Oh, the circus acts were stupendous! There was so much to see. The ferocious lion let out a mighty, bone-rattling roar, and the crowd was instantly silenced. The bravest man on earth, King Eddie, unflinchingly placed his entire head into the lion's mouth! Then the elephants marched in, wearing dazzling headdresses over their gigantic ears. They balanced on balls, rolled over, danced, and even jumped rope.

The clowns, led by Bee-Roll and Dave Zee, made everyone—young and old—laugh so hard that many wet their pants. Then Georgie's Juggling Jesters rode in on their unicycles, tossing all kinds of things into the air: bowling balls and pins, flaming swords, goldfish still in their bowls, and even small children! Only children who volunteered were juggled, of course, but many lined up for a chance to be in the act!

Leading off the high wire was Lancelot Legstrong in yellow, the toughest man on earth. Lance rode his bicycle with great bravado across the high wire—forward, backwards and, not to be believed, upside down. He finished his act by cycling across the high wire, carrying his entire family on his shoulders.

Lancelot was followed by Mario the Marvelous, wearing his signature zebra-striped leotard. Mario thrilled the crowd with his gravity-defying leaps across the wire.

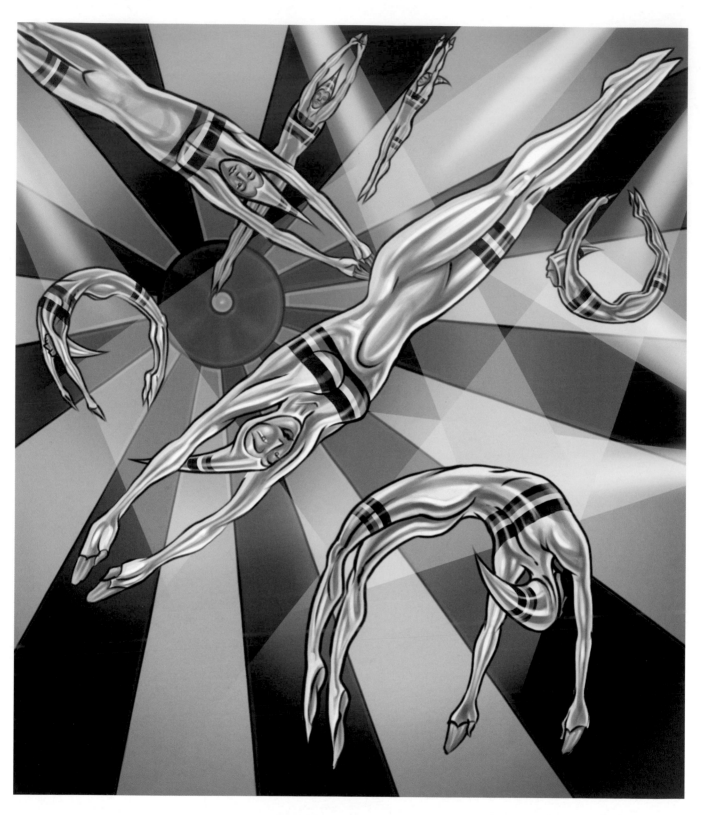

The crowd cheered the loudest when the Flying Boonanas took to the sky. They swung on the high wire, way above everyone's head. Every acrobat showed the incredible grace and strength of a gymnast and moved perfectly in sync with all the other acrobats.

Next, the Boonanas took to the trapeze. They swung back and forth and zoomed every which way in the air. Then they launched themselves into flight toward a waiting partner who grasped their hands just in the nick of time.

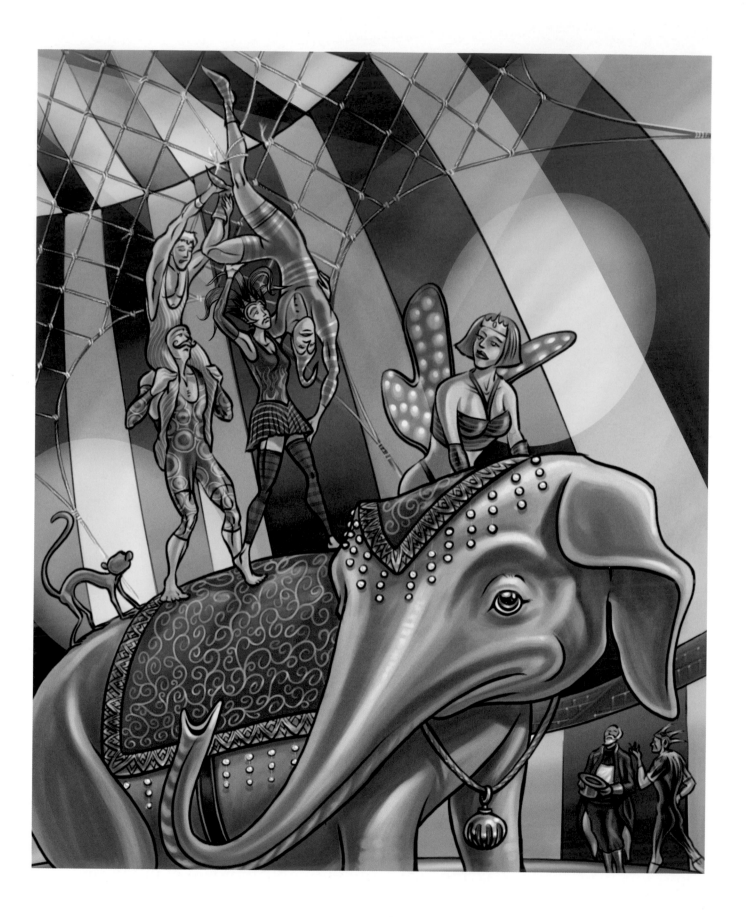

Then, one year the circus rolled into town, but everything had changed. The tent was full of holes and leaked. The organ was out of tune. Even more worrisome, the safety net was worn out. It could no longer catch a fallen trapeze artist. Many had already slipped through big gaping holes and bonked on the ground. The Boonanas and other high wire acts were afraid to perform; some had even quit the act. The circus was in danger of closing its doors forever.

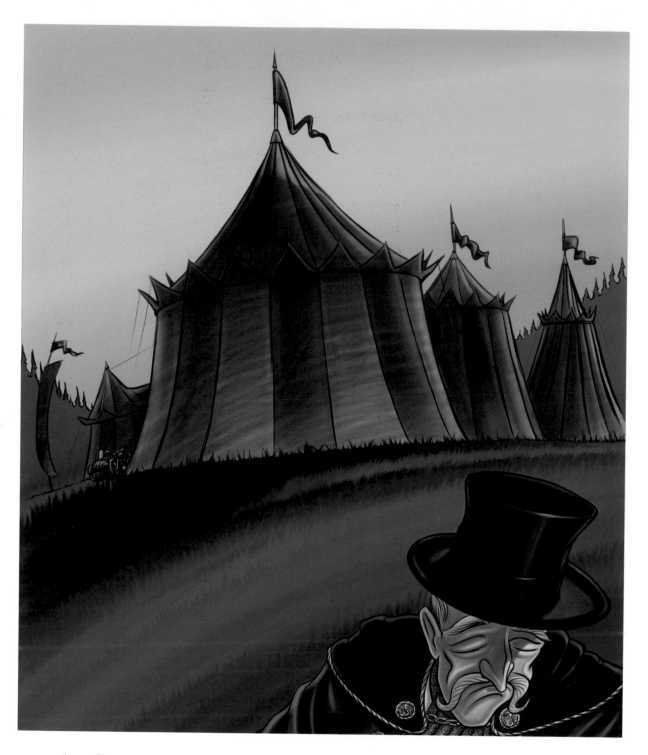

The people of Sweetwater wondered how this could happen, and soon they found out. J. J. Owens, the Circus Ringmaster, was sick with cancer. He didn't have the energy to keep up repairs. The performers were all worried about him, too. After all, they were like a big family. Still, no one knew quite what to do. The townspeople were determined to help. They gathered with the circus performers and came up with a plan.

Everybody volunteered for tasks they were good at doing. Some people cooked meals for J. J. Owens; others drove him to his doctor appointments. The huge mounds of circus laundry were washed and ironed. The tent was patched and sewn. The organ was tuned, and the poles were painted. While J. J. Owens was in the hospital and afterwards, there was always a friend to stay with him and keep him company.

The best idea came from a boy named Max. With everybody's help, Max said, they could fix the safety net. The high wire acts and acrobats could perform again, and the circus would return to its former glory.

And that is exactly what happened. The gracious townspeople of Sweetwater went to work. Each and every person brought a thread to add to the net. Some were long. Some were short. And they came in every color of the rainbow. The people wove together their threads to make a much stronger safety net than ever before! With love and care from family and friends, a Survivorship Net was created.

That is when things really began to change. The acrobats returned to the circus. The Boonanas, Lancelot, and the rest of his high wire family returned. Even Mario came out of retirement to rejoin the circus. The Survivorship Net attracted new acts like Phinneas Davis and his son, Taylor, "The Human Cannonballs." Once again, the J. J. Owens Roundbottom Circus could be called "The Most Amazing Show on Earth!"

Max smiled. It was a good story.

"Dad, was that story real?" Max asked.

His dad nodded. "When the doctors told me that I was sick, I felt just like that strong man carrying his family across the high wire—but without a safety net below us. It did not take long before I found out that I needed help just like the people in the circus story. And just like they did years ago, everybody around us pitched in to add a thread to our 'Survivorship Net.'

"Many people helped me build my Survivorship Net, just like the story said—one thread at a time. First were the many doctors who treated me with such great care. Next were the nurses who were like angels watching over me. And I would have been lost without the loving support of your mom. The many friends who brought us food helped us get through each day.

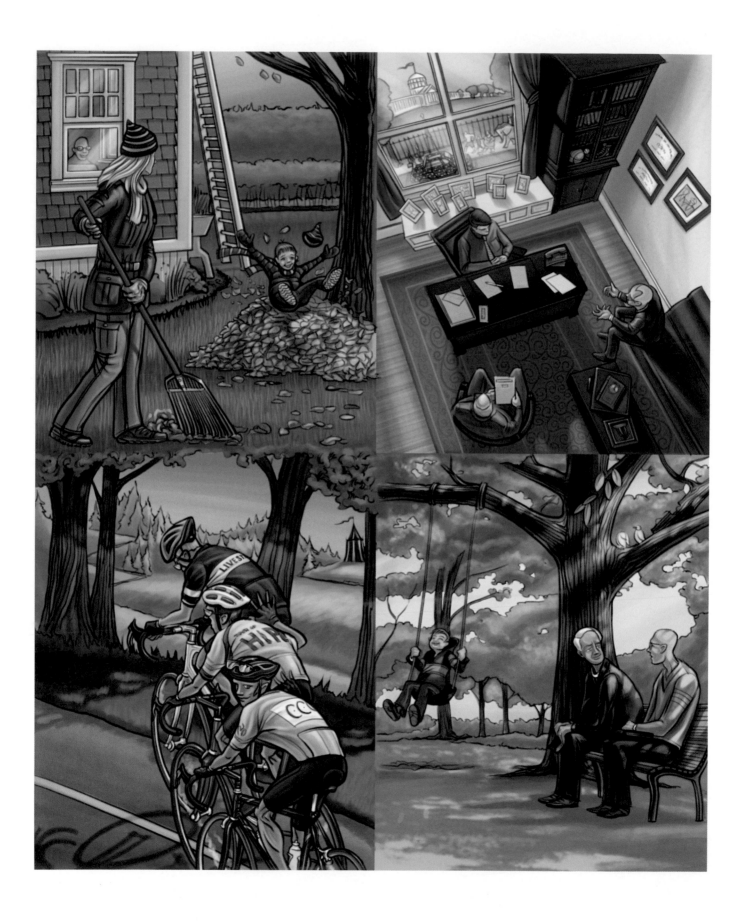

"From raking leaves to lifting things, everyone pitched in to help us. My boss added a thread by giving me a flexible work schedule so I could continue contributing at work. Our congressman and senators added threads with laws to help and protect the rights of patients. Big brother John and my buddies who kept me active weaved in their threads as well. The many people who prayed for healing added threads of faith and hope. Their support boosted our spirits and gave us faith that better days were ahead. And I did what I could to get better and stay healthy like exercising, which works like medicine does."

"Dad, how can I add a thread to The Survivorship Net?"

"Max, you've already added so many, just by being near and helping me and your mom."

"But I want to add more, Dad."

"Okay, Max, let's sit down with Mom tonight and make a list."

"Great, but isn't there something I could do for you right now?"

"Well, Max, I could sure use some company on a bike ride around the block."

In a flash, Max jumped out of his dad's lap and was snapping on his bike helmet before Dad was even out of his chair. As they cruised down the street, Max had a huge smile on his face that stretched from ear to ear.

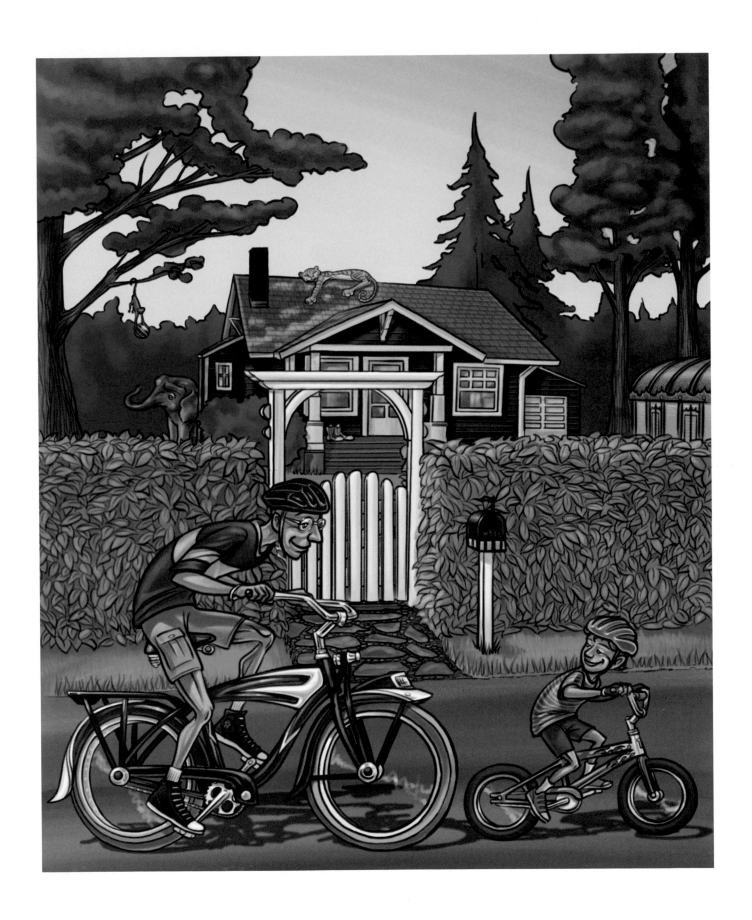

The Survivorship Net has come full circle, and I am returning some of the care and kindness shown to me by adding threads to the Survivorship Net for other people. I give speeches and advocate for better care and patients' rights. I connect with other survivors by phone or by writing messages of support. By sharing my story, I am helping others become survivors just like me. I tell everyone that cancer may slow you down for awhile, but it does not have to run your life. Cancer limits you only if you let it.

Have you added
your thread to the
Survivorship Net?

Afterwords

Jim Owens and son, Max

Jim unknowingly became an advocate for cancer patients after he was diagnosed with an inoperable brain tumor. The time-consuming, often frustrating, process of navigating the available survivor resources led to Jim's mission of cancer outreach and advocacy. I called him my "Cancer Crusader."

Throughout his ten-year battle with cancer, Jim remained physically active, cycling thousands of miles, competing in several marathon Nordic ski races, and swimming to maintain his physical strength. He threw himself into fundraising and outreach for the Lance Armstrong Foundation (LAF) with the same focus, discipline, and commitment as he had for any other endurance event. His efforts were tireless, right up to the very end.

Jim knew firsthand that a group of loving people helping out is vital to survivorship. He was thankful for his large loving family, many friends, and all the people who added threads to his Survivorship Net. This book is his legacy, his final thread in the ever growing Survivorship Net. He never gave up HOPE.

Barb Owens

Jim never gave up. He believed to the end that he would beat this disease. He was driven by his love for and dedication to Barb and Max.

I could never get Jim to slow down at work. I don't know how he did it some days. He would not allow cancer to get in the way of his intense dedication to our company.

More than once, throughout the countless doctors' appointments and MRIs, it seemed we were reaching the end. Jim wouldn't hear of it. He was constantly searching for new treatment options. More than one clinical trial Jim was on is now a standard protocol. Jim broke ground—not only for his own survival, but for those to follow.

This book was a labor of love that Jim worked on until his last day. His vast network of friends and family are a part of every page, which Bill Cass has so brilliantly illustrated.

I miss Jim dearly, but his message of HOPE will never die.

Livestrong.

John Owens

From the Illustrator

Jim and I first met at the Ride for the Roses* in Austin, Texas. We took our picture together at the start of the ride and chatted a bit before the ride really cranked up. I was immediately struck by Jim's big smile and honesty. The internal strength he revealed when talking about his disease was truly inspiring.

Bill Cass (left) with Jim Owens

A couple of years passed. One day the phone rang, and it was Jim, telling me he had written a story and he wanted me to illustrate it. When I read the manuscript, I knew he had something unique: a clear and simple way to tell his six-year-old why he didn't feel well. I showed it to my wife and she said, "You have to do this."

The work began slowly at first, but then the book started to take shape. Jim and I had some long discussions over the phone, including a disagreement about how to deal with the "faith" aspect of the book. It forced me to look outside my own opinions, as well as solicit the opinions of others on the subject. I learned a great deal through those discussions.

The book slowly moved forward, and Jim called again to see if we could meet in person. He was very excited. The American Cancer Society wanted to publish the book. He was up in Seattle, so we planned to meet in Olympia,

Washington. I was proud to show him the progress I had made, but was taken aback when I saw him. By that time, it was evident that his cancer had taken a strong hold on him. We made plans to really get this project going, and I promised to have all the illustrations done by January 1, 2009.

One of the things we talked about was the possibility of having Lance Armstrong write the foreword for the book. I called Lance's friend and agent, Bart, and sent him the manuscript. A month later, I had all the sketches dialed in and was ready to do the finishes. I tried to contact Jim a few weeks before Christmas to give him an update, but he didn't return my call. This was very unlike him, and it made me nervous. He called a week later to tell me he was having a tough time. I kept my focus on the goal of finishing the illustrations by the first of the year.

I called Jim one night and although he was really struggling, he wanted to know about Lance and that foreword. Barb got on the phone and gave me the update. Jim had taken a bad turn, and there were no more medical options.

I focused on what I could do and called Bart the next day. He told me Lance was going to write the foreword. I excitedly called back and talked to Jim very briefly. Barb and I talked again, too, and she told me he was really close. I called Bart back to ask if there was any way Lance could call Jim. I was not the only one.

On the Friday after New Year's Day, Lance called Jim to talk for awhile. Jim was lucid, and they had a great chat. Lance told Jim about all the phone calls he had received on Jim's behalf. Lance also told Jim he would be writing the foreword.

On Sunday, my phone rang and it was John, Jim's brother. The moment I heard his voice, I knew why. Jim had passed that morning. John and I talked about how Jim had really hung on just to make sure that Lance would be part of it.

My hardest moment was when I sat at my drawing table to finish the last two illustrations. I just stared at the screen for over an hour before I began. Once I started, I don't even remember time passing. As I worked on the last drawing of Jim and Max riding together, the strangest thing happened. I started to laugh out loud. I wasn't really in a laughing mood until I realized it was the joyful way one laughs when he goes around the block for a bike ride with his son.

Jim, you will be missed.

Bill Cass

* The Ride for the Roses Weekend is an invitational bike event for top fundraisers of the LIVESTRONG Challenge. The LIVESTRONG Challenge is the signature fundraising event for the Lance Armstrong Foundation (LAF) and is held annually in Austin, Texas.

Jim Owens passed away on January 4, 2009, after a ten-year battle with brain cancer.

About the Author

Jim Owens was an engineer and businessman from Minneapolis, Minnesota. With his brother John, he ran Owens Companies, a fifty-year-old engineering and contracting firm founded by their father. Jim was a ten-year brain cancer survivor. He and his wife, Barbara, had a son, Max, now ten years old. It was Max's innocent questions about his dad's disease that inspired this book.

Jim was an avid cyclist, triathlete, swimmer, runner, and Nordic skier. A long-time supporter of the Lance Armstrong Foundation (LAF), he received the Triumph Award from the LAF in 2005. As a member of the 2004 Tour of Hope National Team, Jim and nineteen others from the cancer community, along with Lance Armstrong, rode 3,500 miles from Los Angeles to Washington, D.C., in less than nine days to promote cancer research and clinical trial participation. Jim chronicled his cancer journey on his Web site: **www.jimsjourney.com.**

About the Illustrator

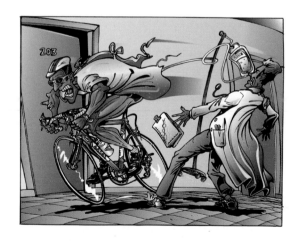

Bill Cass recently left his 14-year career as a footwear designer for Nike and moved to Whidbey Island in Washington State to open a design studio and retail shop with his wife, Sam. They have two daughters, Tabatha and Izzy. With this "throwing caution to the wind" move, they are chasing a dream that was, to a very large extent, inspired by meeting Jim and working on this project with him and his family.

Bill is a longtime supporter of the Lance Armstrong Foundation (LAF). Along with designing Lance's cycling shoe for the seven Tour de France wins, Bill illustrated and designed the first ten posters used for the Ride for the Roses, an event held annually in conjunction with LAF's LIVESTRONG Challenge Austin. The first poster was a get-well card he made for Lance during his battle with cancer and is credited as being the inspiration for the Ride for the Roses.